The Pirate
Who Said
Please

Timothy Knapman

Illustrated by Jimothy Oliver

QED Publishing

Pirate Jim is a **pirate king**
who rules the seven seas.

But Jim is very **well-behaved**,
and never forgets to say
please.

Just one look at his cardboard sword
and all the sharks **shiver** and **shake**.

But he always says,
"Thank you, Granny!"
when she gives him biscuits or cake.

His **pirate ship** is a scary sight,
the terror of the sitting room!

But he remembered to say, "Hey, Mum,
please may I borrow the chair and broom?"

Pirate Jim **loves** a pirate feast –
it's his favourite **pirate treat!**

But he never forgets to ask **nicely**
if he wants some more to eat.

He captures lots of **treasure chests**
without a fuss or a fight.
You see, people give him lots of things...

...because he's so **polite**.

But Pirate Jim **wasn't always nice**
to the rest of his pirate crew.

He was **rude** and **mean** and hosed them down until they were all soaked through.

He **snatched** whichever toys they brought
before the games had begun.

So the next time they **didn't bring any**,
and the games weren't half as much fun.

At parties he'd forever be shouting,
"More pirate food for me!"

So people thought, "What a **rude** little pirate!"
and didn't invite him to tea.

When he told his crew what to do,
he **wouldn't** say **"please"** - he'd **moan!**

So they left him behind on an island –
far away and all **alone**.

And that's how **Pirate Jim** was taught
the most important lesson you'll learn:
be **polite** to other people
and they'll be polite in **return**.

So take note, you scurvy dogs,
of the tale of **Pirate Jim**.
If you want to be a pirate king,
then you must **behave** like him.

Always say "**please**" when you're asking,
and always **remember to thank**.
Or you'll make the pirates angry,
and you'll have to walk the **plank!**

Next steps

☠ Ask your child what they know about pirates. Do they know where pirates live or what kind of clothes they wear? Then, look at the first few pages of the book and ask them to describe the pictures on each page.

☠ Ask your child to describe the situations when Jim says "please" and "thank you". Tell your child that it's important to say "please" if they ask for a favour or would like to have something, and to say "thank you" when they are given what they ask for. You could give some examples or do a role-play to illustrate when to say "please" and "thank you".

☠ Ask your child why they think other people give Jim what he wants.

☠ In the past Jim didn't have a lot of fun playing with his friends and probably felt sad that they did not invite him to tea. His friends even left him alone on an island. Discuss why Jim's friends treated him this way.

☠ Discuss the picture at the end where Jim and his friends are playing together again. What are the 'pirates' in the picture doing and how do they feel? Discuss with your child whether they like to play with friends or play alone. Talk about how being polite makes it more fun to play with others. Ask your child to draw a picture of themselves playing with their friends.

☠ Emphasize that people will treat you the way you treat them. For example, if you are polite to other people, they will be polite to you.

Consultant: Cecilia A. Essau
Professor of Developmental
Psychopathology
Director of the Centre for Applied
Research and Assessment in Child and
Adolescent Wellbeing, Roehampton
University, London

Editor: Alexandra Koken
Designer: Andrew Crowson

Copyright © QED Publishing 2012

First published in the UK in 2012 by
QED Publishing
A Quarto Group company
230 City Road
London EC1V 2TT

www.qed-publishing.co.uk

A catalogue record for this book is available from the British Library.

ISBN 978 1 84835 897 3

Printed in China